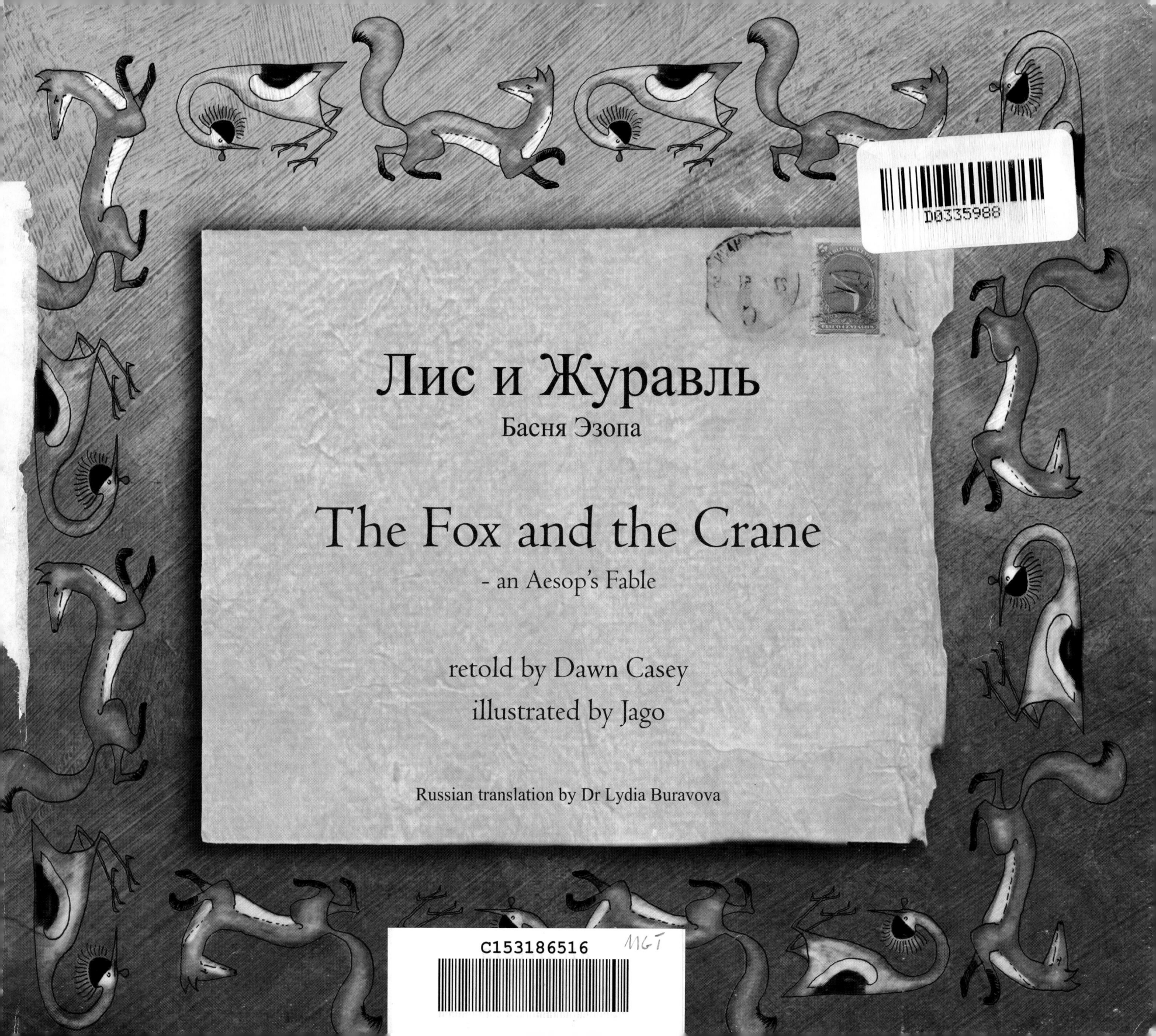

Лис и Журавль

Басня Эзопа

The Fox and the Crane

- an Aesop's Fable

retold by Dawn Casey

illustrated by Jago

Russian translation by Dr Lydia Buravova

D0335988

C153186516 MGT

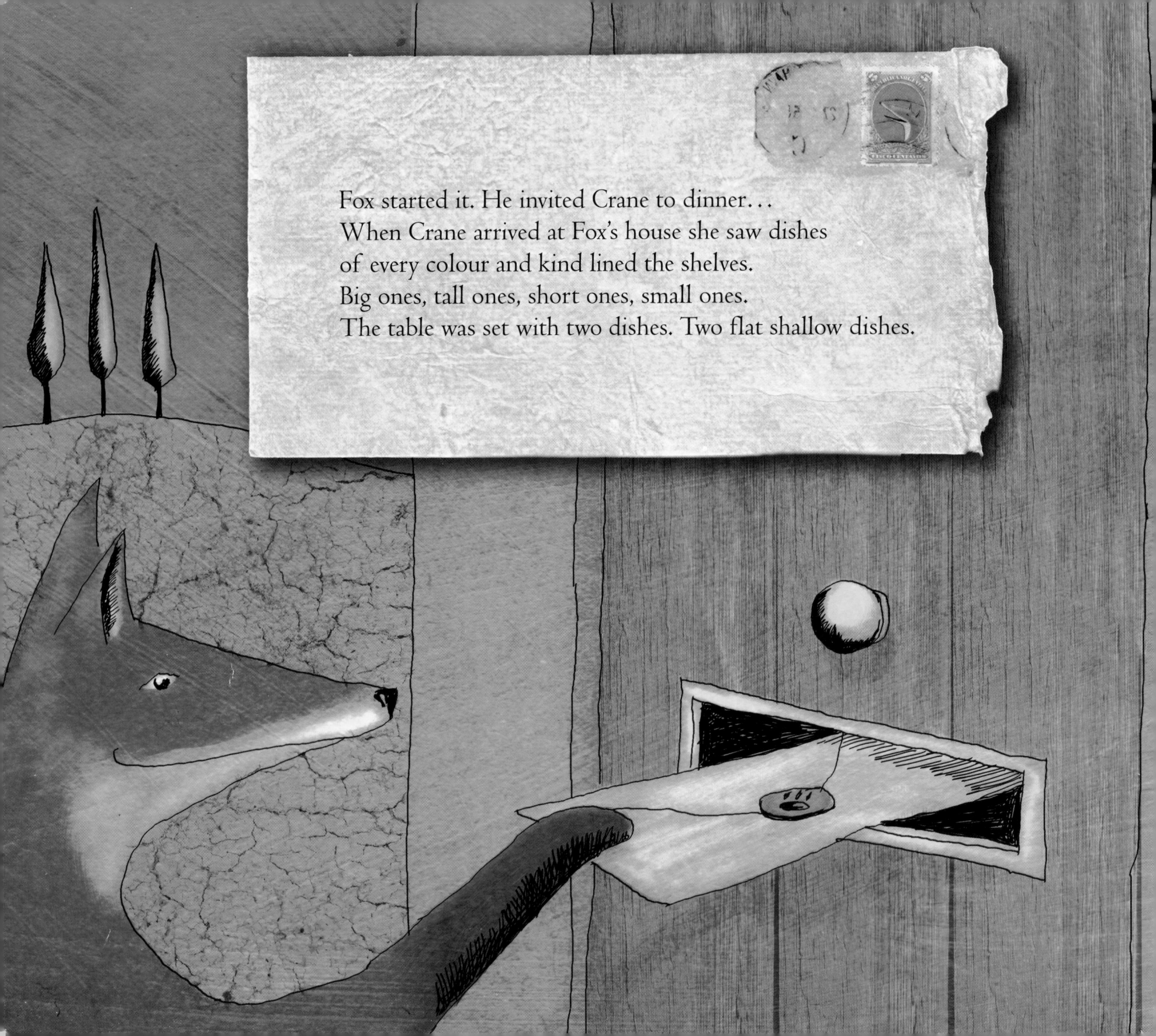

Fox started it. He invited Crane to dinner…
When Crane arrived at Fox's house she saw dishes
of every colour and kind lined the shelves.
Big ones, tall ones, short ones, small ones.
The table was set with two dishes. Two flat shallow dishes.

Начал всё это Лис. Он позвал Журавля на обед...
Приходит Журавль в дом Лиса и видит на полках посуду всевозможных цветов и размеров. Миски, кувшины, мелкие тарелки и маленькие.
Стол накрыт на двоих. На столе – две плоские мелкие тарелки.

Журавль клевал, стуча по тарелке длиным тонким клювом.
Однако, как он ни старался, в рот не попало ни глотка супа.

Crane pecked and she picked with her long thin beak. But no matter how hard she tried she could not get even a sip of the soup.

Лис видел, что у Журавля ничего не получается, но только хихикал. Он поднёс свой суп к губам и, громко чавкая, вылакал его.

«Ах, как вкусно!», - усмехнулся он, вытирая усы лапой.

«Что же ты, Журавль, не притронулся к супу», - сказал Лис с ухмылкой. «Как ЖАЛЬ, что он тебе не понравился», - добавил он, давясь от смеха.

Fox watched Crane struggling and sniggered. He lifted his own soup to his lips, and with a SIP, SLOP, SLURP he lapped it all up. "Ahhhh, delicious!" he scoffed, wiping his whiskers with the back of his paw.

"Oh Crane, you haven't touched your soup," said Fox with a smirk. "I AM sorry you didn't like it," he added, trying not to snort with laughter.

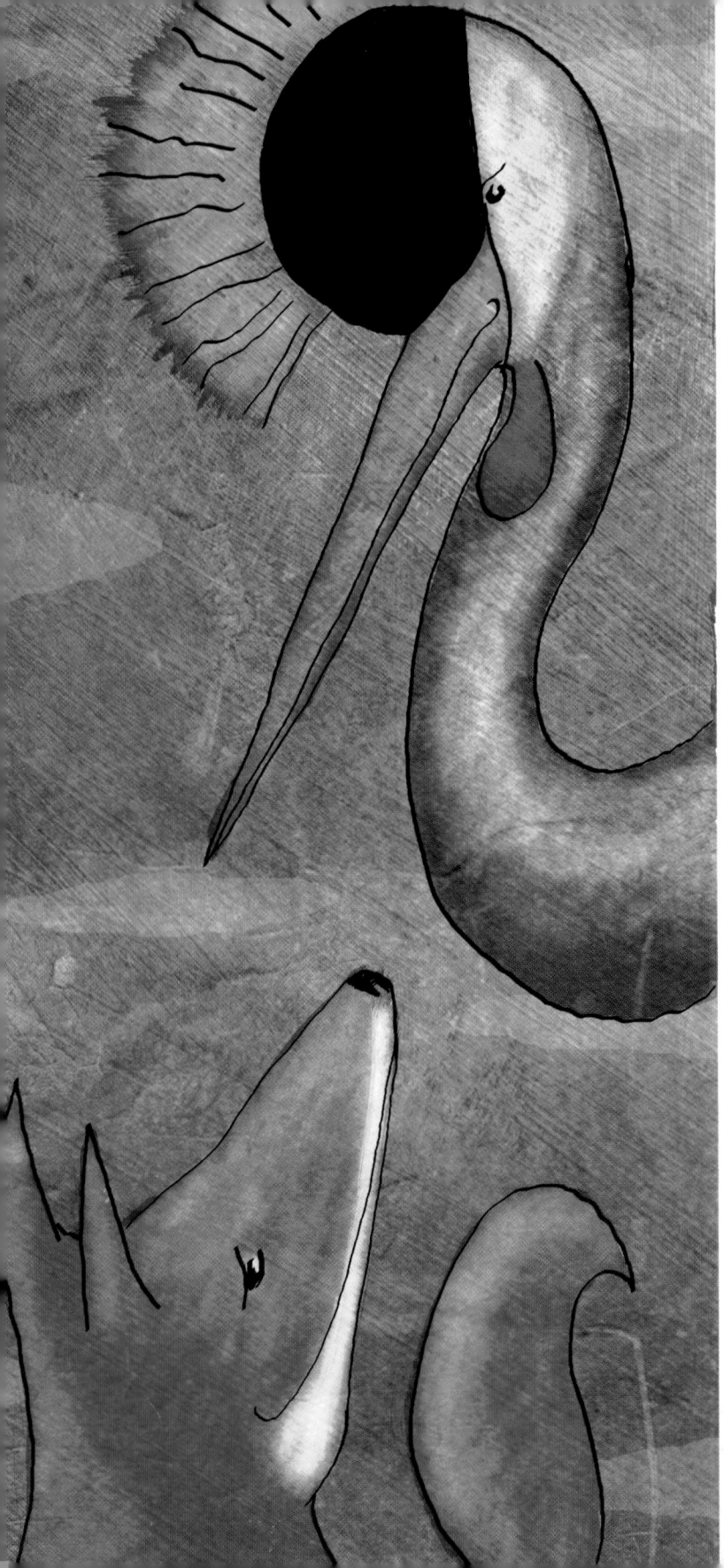

Журавль на это ничего не ответил. Он посмотрел на тарелку. Затем посмотрел на Лиса и улыбнулся. «Уважаемый Лис, благодарю за гостеприимство, - сказал вежливо Журавль. - Позволь мне отплатить тебе тем же – приходи ко мне домой на обед».

Когда Лис пришёл к Журавлю, окно в доме было открыто. Из окна струился аппетитный запах. Принюхиваясь, Лис поднял морду. У него потекли слюнки. В животе забурчало.
Он облизнулся.

Crane said nothing. She looked at the meal. She looked at the dish. She looked at Fox, and smiled.
"Dear Fox, thank you for your kindness," said Crane politely. "Please let me repay you – come to dinner at my house."

When Fox arrived the window was open. A delicious smell drifted out. Fox lifted his snout and sniffed. His mouth watered. His stomach rumbled. He licked his lips.

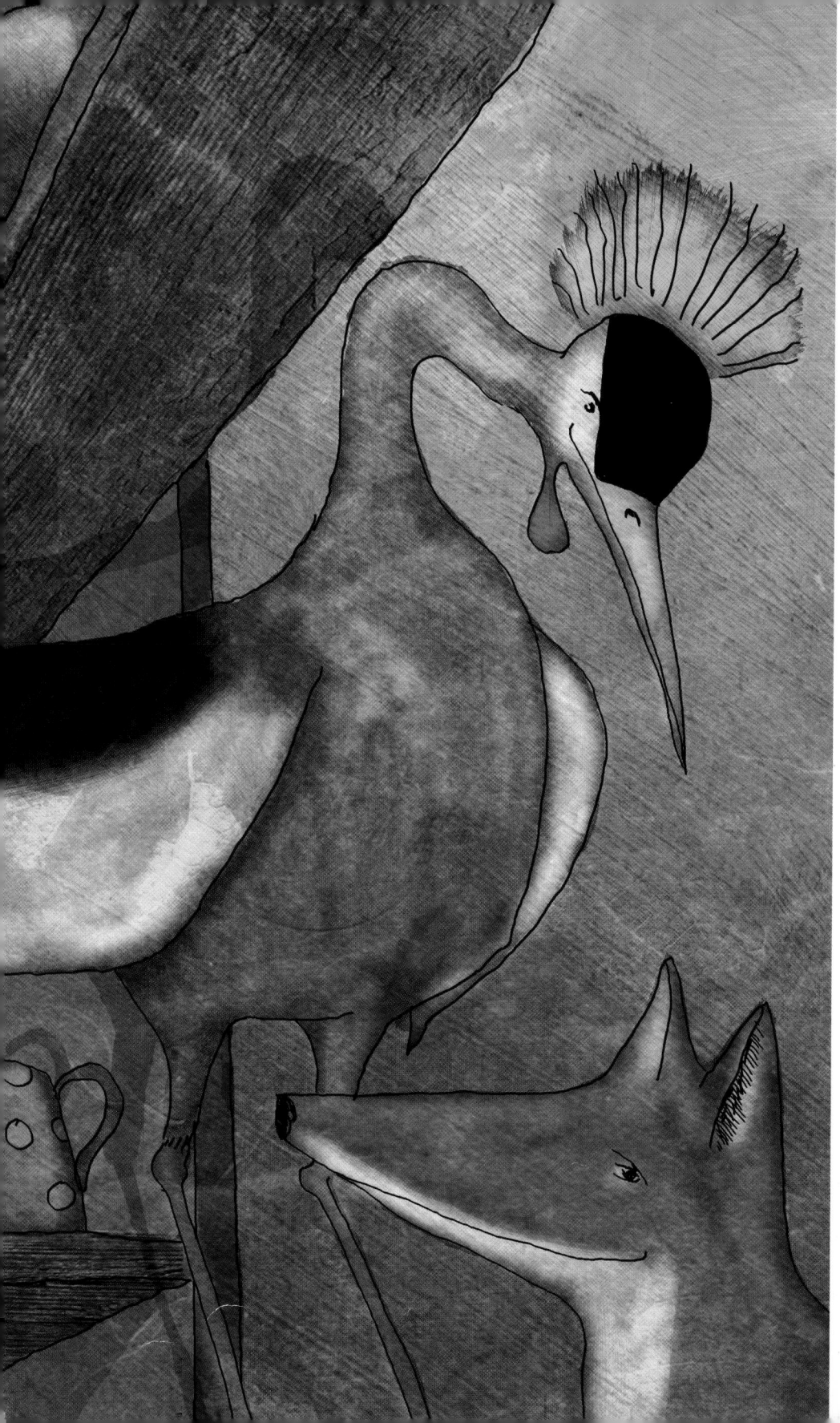

«Добро пожаловать, уважаемый Лис»,
- сказал Журавль, приглашая войти.
Лис поспешил в дом. Он увидел на
полках посуду всевозможных цветов
и размеров. Красную, синюю, старую,
новую.
Стол был накрыт на двоих. На столе
– два кувшина с узким горлышком.

"My dear Fox, do come in," said Crane,
extending her wing graciously.
Fox pushed past. He saw dishes of
every colour and kind lined the shelves.
Red ones, blue ones, old ones, new ones.
The table was set with two dishes.
Two tall narrow dishes.

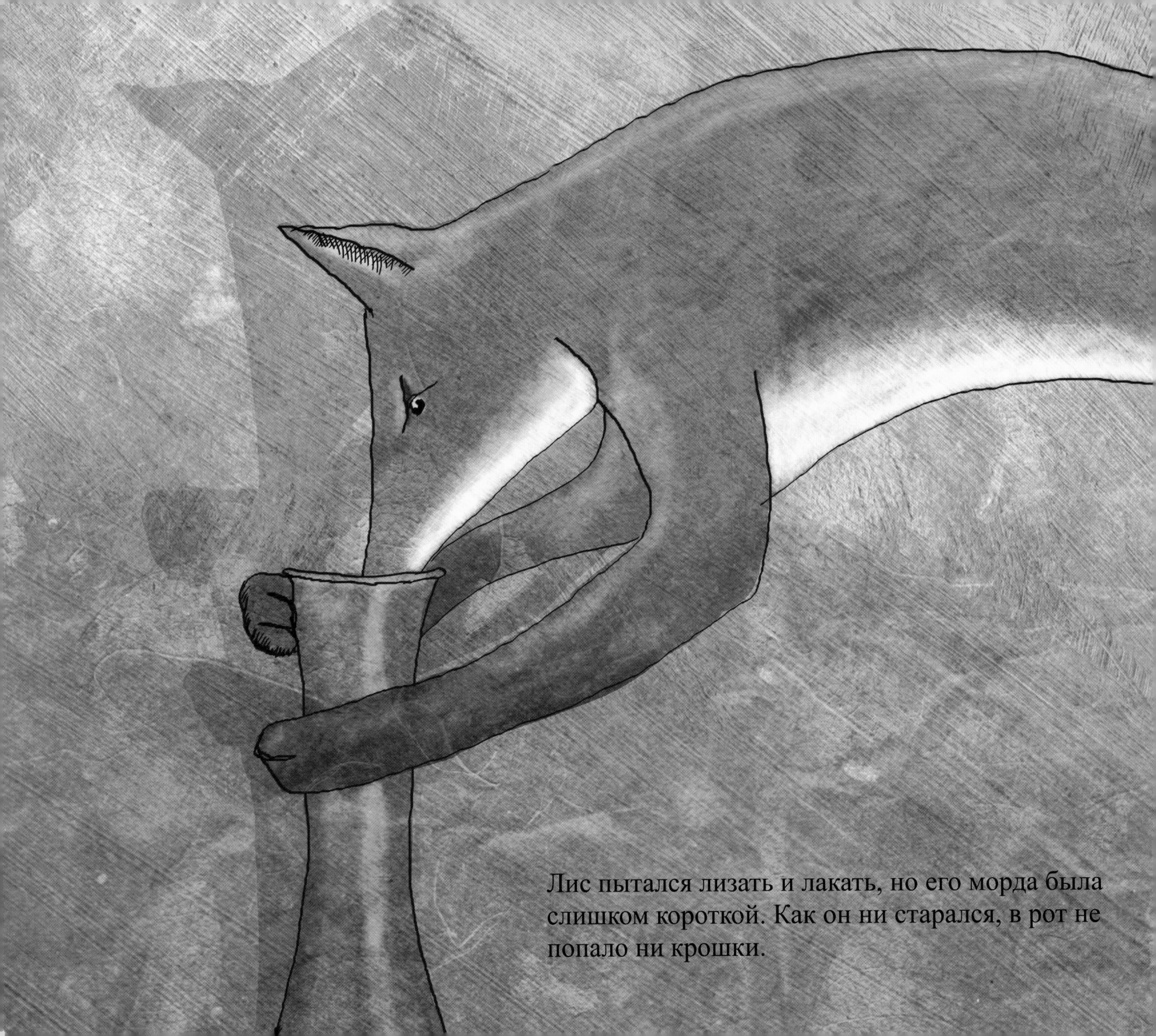

Лис пытался лизать и лакать, но его морда была слишком короткой. Как он ни старался, в рот не попало ни крошки.

Fox licked and he lapped with his short little snout.
But no matter how hard he tried he could not
get even a mouthful of the meal.

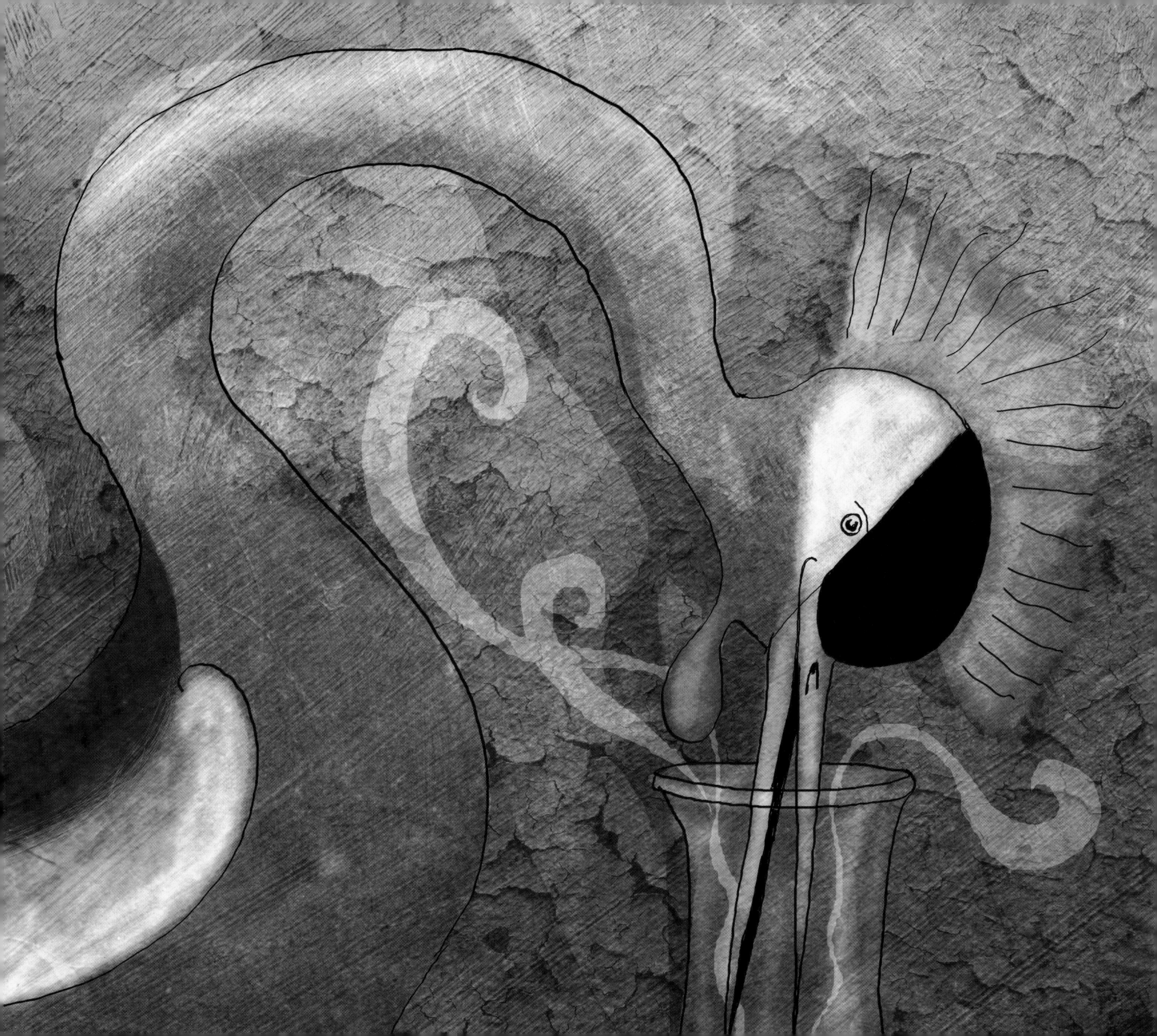

Журавль же ел обед, не спеша, смакуя каждый кусочек.
«Уважаемый Лис, спасибо за то, что ты пришёл, - улыбнулся он, – приятно отплатить тебе за твоё гостеприимство».

В животе Лиса забурчало ещё громче.
И пошёл он домой, несолоно хлебавши.

Crane ate her meal very slowly, savouring every mouthful.
"Dear Fox, thank you so much for coming," she smiled,
"it has been a pleasure to repay your kindness."

Fox's tummy gurgled and grumbled.
And when he went home, he was still hungry.

The Fox and the Crane

Writing Activity:
Read the story. Explain that we can write our own fable by changing the characters.

Discuss the different animals you could use, bearing in mind what different kinds of dishes they would need! For example, instead of the fox and the crane you could have a tiny mouse and a tall giraffe.

Write an example together as a class, then give the children the opportunity to write their own. Children who need support could be provided with a writing frame.

Art Activity:
Dishes of every colour and kind! Create them from clay, salt dough, play dough… Make them, paint them, decorate them…

Maths Activity:
Provide a variety of vessels: bowls, jugs, vases, mugs… Children can use these to investigate capacity:

Compare the containers and order them from smallest to largest.

Estimate the capacity of each container.

Young children can use non-standard measures e.g. 'about 3 beakers full'.

Check estimates by filling the container with coloured liquid ('soup') or dry lentils.

Older children can use standard measures such as a litre jug, and measure using litres and millilitres. How near were the estimates?

Label each vessel with its capacity.

The King of the Forest

Writing Activity:
Children can write their own fables by changing the setting of this story. Think about what kinds of animals you would find in a different setting. For example how about 'The King of the Arctic' starring an arctic fox and a polar bear!

Storytelling Activity:
Draw a long path down a roll of paper showing the route Fox took through the forest. The children can add their own details, drawing in the various scenes and re-telling the story orally with model animals.

If you are feeling ambitious you could chalk the path onto the playground so that children can act out the story using appropriate noises and movements! (They could even make masks to wear, decorated with feathers, woollen fur, sequin scales etc.)

Music Activity:
Children choose a forest animal. Then select an instrument that will make a sound that matches the way their animal looks and moves. Encourage children to think about musical features such as volume, pitch and rhythm. For example a loud, low, plodding rhythm played on a drum could represent an elephant.

Children perform their animal sounds. Can the class guess the animal?

Children can play their pieces in groups, to create a forest soundscape.

Лесной Царь

Китайская басня

The King of the Forest

- a Chinese Fable

retold by Dawn Casey

illustrated by Jago

Russian translation by

Dr Lydia Buravova

Как-то раз гулял Лис по лесу. Вдруг слышит, как в высокой траве что-то шевелится.

ШОРОХ Нечто большое.
МОРГНУЛО Нечто желтоглазое.
СВЕРКНУЛО Нечто с зубами, отстрыми как нож.

Fox was walking in the forest when he heard something moving in the long grass.

RUSTLE Something big.
BLINK Something with yellow eyes.
FLASH Something with teeth like knives.

«Доброе утро, маленький Лис», - ухмыльнулся Тигр, показывая зубы.
У Лиса перехватило дыхание.
«Рад тебя видеть, - промурлыкал Тигр. - Мне как раз захотелось перекусить».
Лис не замешкался с ответом. «Как ты смеешь! - говорит он. - Разве ты не знаешь, что я – Лесной Царь!»
«Ты! Лесной Царь?» - сказал Тигр и покатился со смеху.
«Если ты не веришь мне, - с достоинством ответил Лис, – иди за мной и ты увидишь, что меня все боятся».
«А это мы ещё посмотрим»,- сказал Тигр.
Итак, Лис пошёл по лесу. А за ним, задрав хвост, гордо последовал Тигр, как вдруг...

"Good morning little fox," Tiger grinned, and his mouth was nothing but teeth.
Fox gulped.
"I am pleased to meet you," Tiger purred. "I was just beginning to feel hungry."
Fox thought fast. "How dare you!" he said. "Don't you know I'm the King of the Forest?"
"You! King of the Forest?" said Tiger, and he roared with laughter.
"If you don't believe me," replied Fox with dignity, "walk behind me and you'll see – everyone is scared of me."
"This I've got to see," said Tiger.
So Fox strolled through the forest. Tiger followed behind proudly, with his tail held high, until…

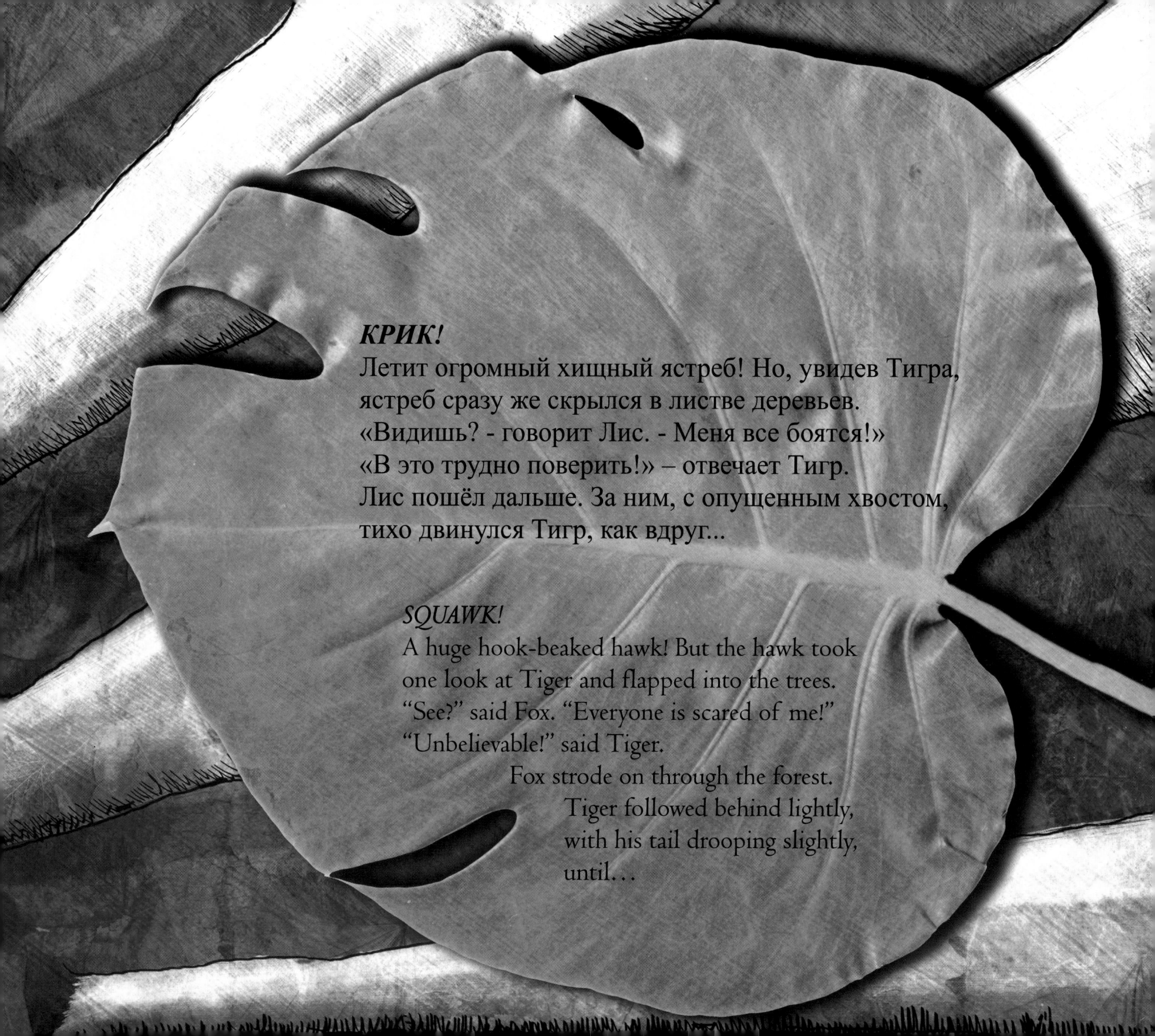

КРИК!
Летит огромный хищный ястреб! Но, увидев Тигра,
ястреб сразу же скрылся в листве деревьев.
«Видишь? - говорит Лис. - Меня все боятся!»
«В это трудно поверить!» – отвечает Тигр.
Лис пошёл дальше. За ним, с опущенным хвостом,
тихо двинулся Тигр, как вдруг...

SQUAWK!
A huge hook-beaked hawk! But the hawk took
one look at Tiger and flapped into the trees.
"See?" said Fox. "Everyone is scared of me!"
"Unbelievable!" said Tiger.
Fox strode on through the forest.
Tiger followed behind lightly,
with his tail drooping slightly,
until...

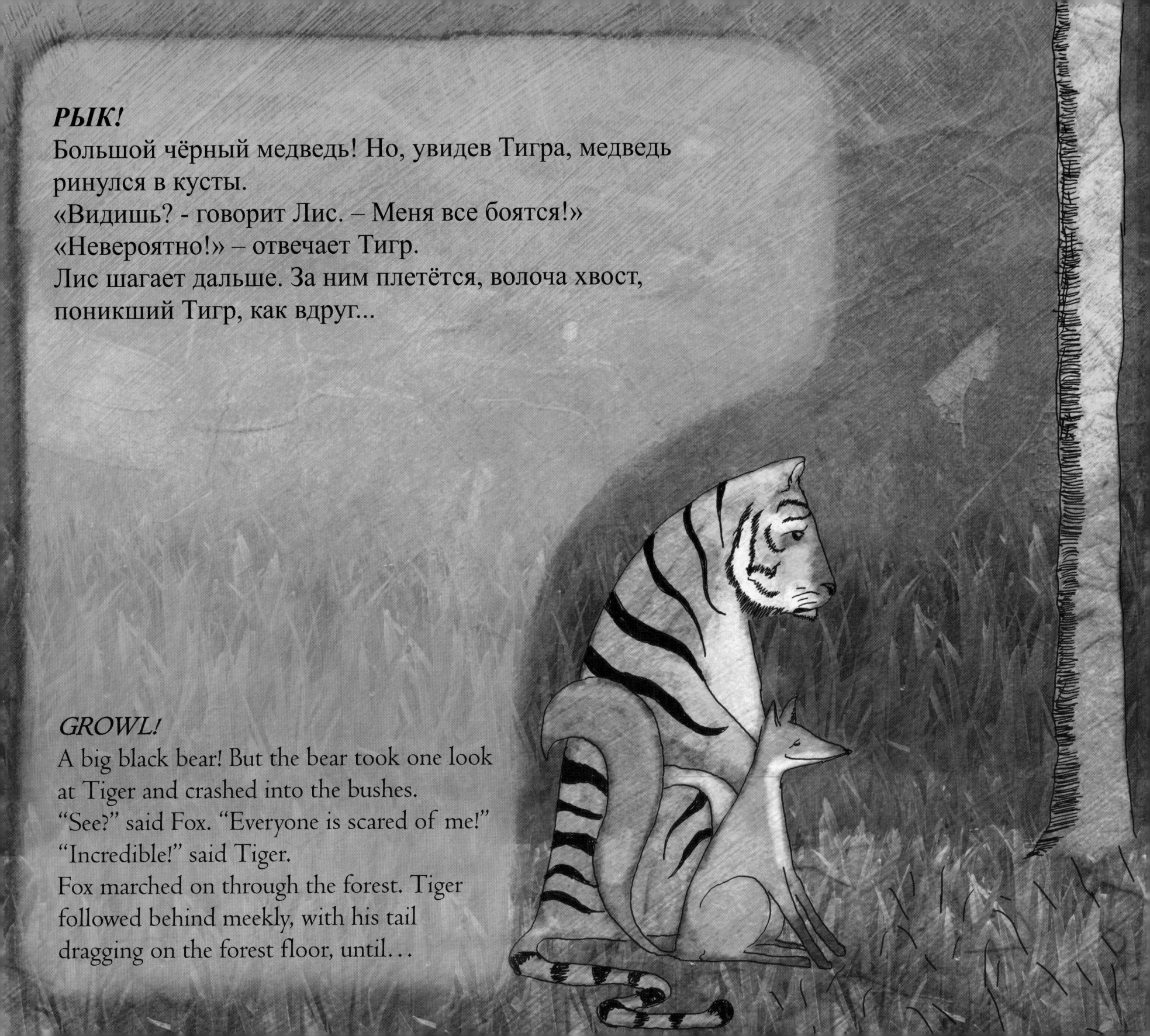

РЫК!
Большой чёрный медведь! Но, увидев Тигра, медведь ринулся в кусты.
«Видишь? - говорит Лис. – Меня все боятся!»
«Невероятно!» – отвечает Тигр.
Лис шагает дальше. За ним плетётся, волоча хвост, поникший Тигр, как вдруг...

GROWL!
A big black bear! But the bear took one look at Tiger and crashed into the bushes.
"See?" said Fox. "Everyone is scared of me!"
"Incredible!" said Tiger.
Fox marched on through the forest. Tiger followed behind meekly, with his tail dragging on the forest floor, until…

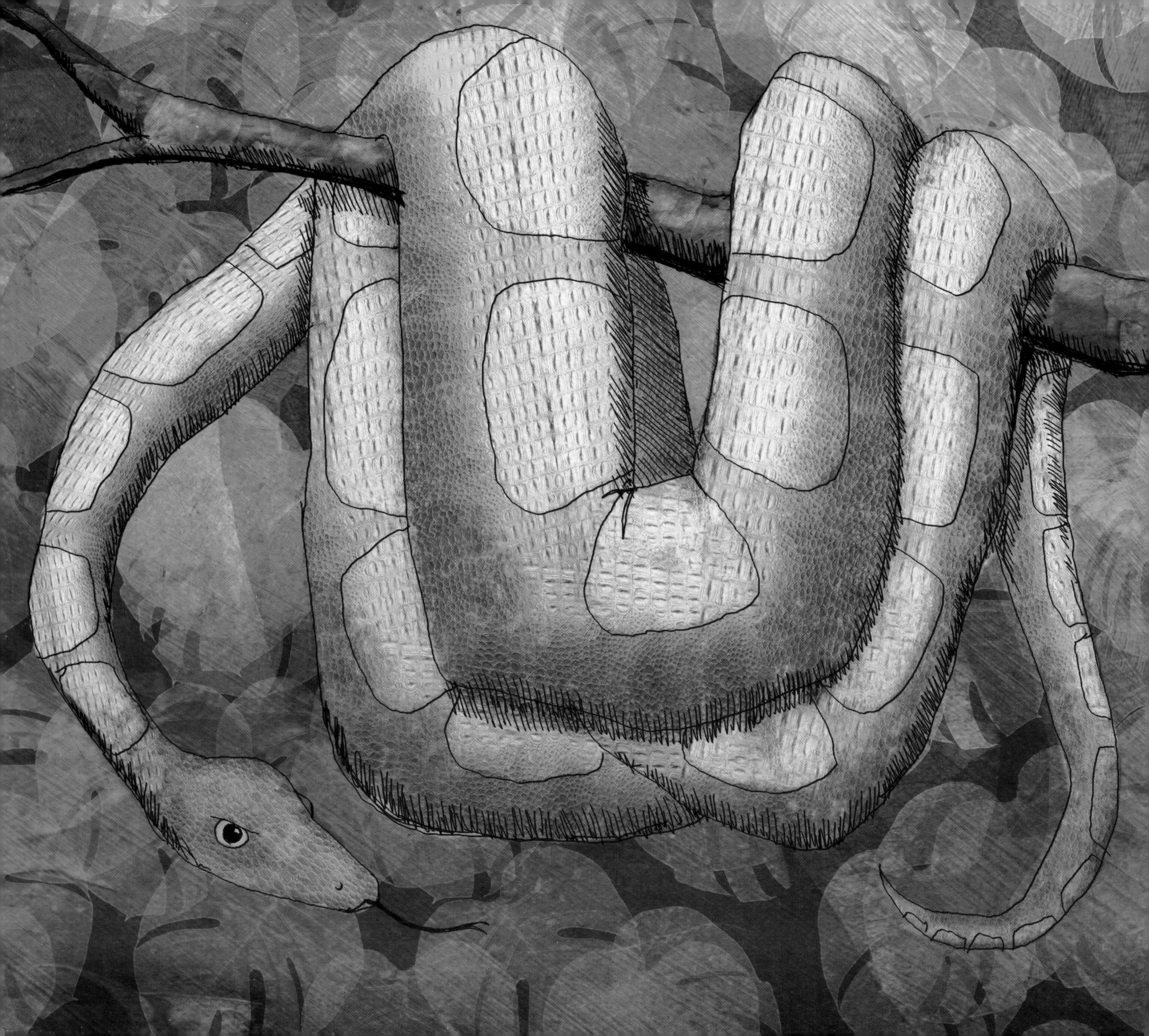

ШИП!
Извивается блестящая змея! Но, увидев Тигра,
змея в мгновение ока уползла в заросли.
«ВИДИШЬ? - говорит Лис. – МЕНЯ ВСЕ БОЯТСЯ!»

HISSSSSSS!
A slinky slidey snake! But the snake took one look
at Tiger and slithered into the undergrowth.
"SEE?" said Fox. "EVERYONE IS SCARED
OF ME!"

«Теперь я и сам вижу, - сказал Тигр. – Ты и, правда, - Лесной Царь,
а я - твой покорный слуга».
«Вот именно, - говорит Лис. – Тогда оставь меня!»

И, поджав хвост, Тигр пошёл восвояси.

"I do see," said Tiger, "you are the King of the Forest and I am your humble servant."
"Good," said Fox. "Then, be gone!"

And Tiger went, with his tail between his legs.

«Лесной Царь», - с улыбкой сказал сам себе Лис. Улыбнувшись, он усмехнулся, а потом не удержался и захихикал, да так и прохохотал всю дорогу домой.

"King of the Forest," said Fox to himself with a smile. His smile grew into a grin, and his grin grew into a giggle, and Fox laughed out loud all the way home.

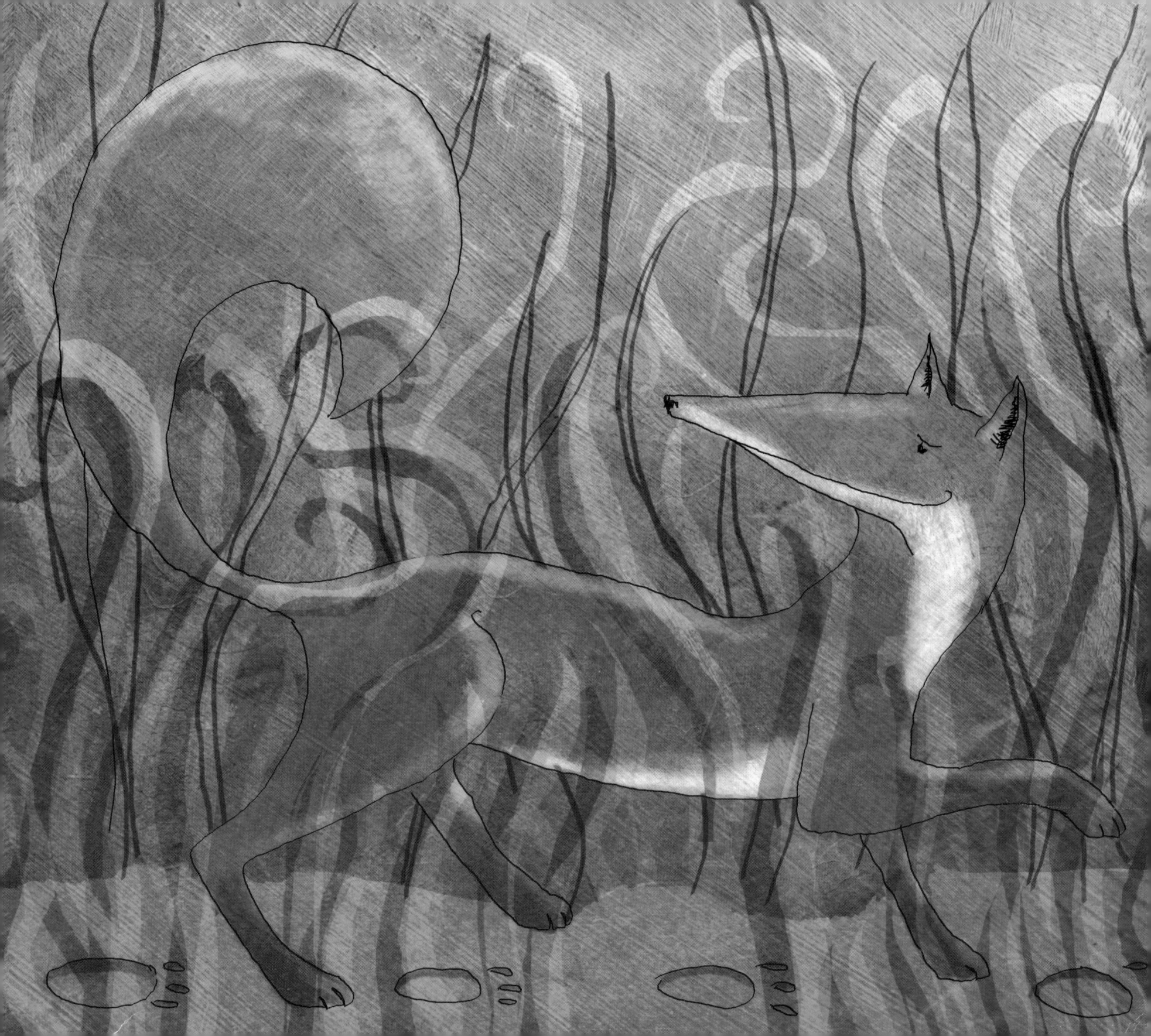

To my Nana, with love - DC
For my wife, Alex - J

First published in 2006 by Mantra Lingua Ltd
Global House, 303 Ballards Lane
London N12 8NP
www.mantralingua.com

Text copyright © 2006 Dawn Casey
Illustration copyright © 2006 Jago
Dual language copyright © Mantra Lingua Ltd
All rights reserved

A CIP record for this book is available from the British Library